FAIRNESS

by Sandra Ziegler
illustrated by Helen Endres

THE CHILD'S WORLD

Mankato, MN 56001

How do you like to go up in a swing,
  Up in the air so blue?
Oh, I do think it the pleasantest thing
  Ever a child can do!

Up in the air and over the wall,
  Till I can see so wide,
Rivers and trees and cattle and all
  Over the countryside—

Till I look down on the garden green,
  Down on the roof so brown—
Up in the air I go flying again,
  Up in the air and down!

—Robert Louis Stevenson

Library of Congress Cataloging-in-Publication Data

Ziegler, Sandra, 1938-
  Fairness.

  Summary: Presents, in simple text and illustrations,
a variety of familiar situations that explain the
concept of fairness.
  1. Fairness—Juvenile literature.   [1. Fairness.
2. Conduct of life]   I. Endres, Helen, ill.   II. Title.
BJ1533.F2Z53   1989   179'.9   88-18976
ISBN 0-89565-390-7

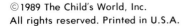

What is fairness? Fairness is taking
turns when there is only one swing.

After you and your sister build a
rainy-day tunnel with chairs, . . .

fairness is putting the chairs away
together.

When two "goblins" come
to your door on Halloween,
fairness is giving each of them
equal treats.

Fairness is taking turns being the
audience when you and your sister
play with puppets.

And fairness is giving your bucket to
your friend because you sat on his
and broke it.

Lining up behind the starting line at
the race—so you all start from the
same place—that's fairness.

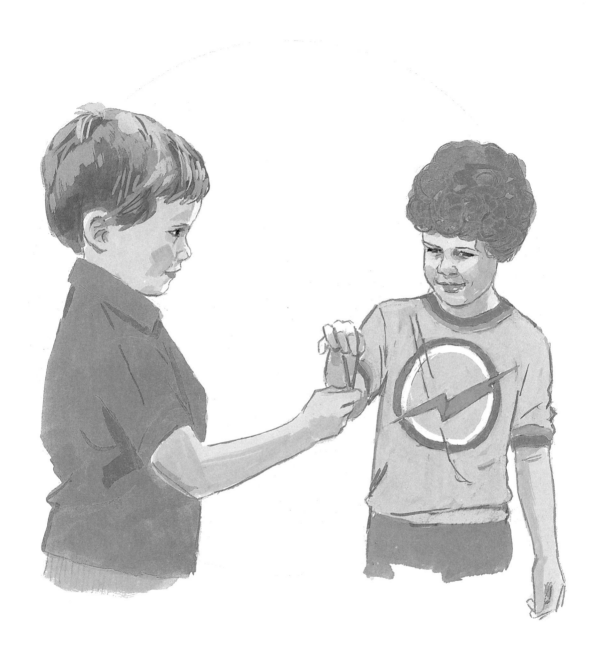

And fairness is drawing straws before
you play tag, to see who will be "It"
first.

When you and your sister get ten
tickets each to spend on the amuse-
ment-park rides, fairness is not asking
for your sister's after you have used
yours.

After a picnic in the park, fairness is cleaning off the picnic table so another family can use it.

In the morning, when Mom has to pack lunches, fix breakfast, and get off to work herself, . . . fairness is getting up when she calls.

At school, fairness is waiting your turn to put the picture you made of yourself on the special birthday train.

21

If your friend lets you ride on his Big Wheel, fairness is letting him play with your ball.

When your sister and you share a dog,
fairness is taking turns teaching him
tricks.

When the ice-cream truck comes
down your street, fairness is waiting
your turn to buy an ice-cream bar.

If you sat beside Dad on the way to the circus and your sister sits there on the way home—that's fairness.

Fairness is playing a game by the
rules . . .

and not calling your sister a ''cheat''
when she honestly wins.

Being fair is being a kind, responsible person. It's practicing the Golden Rule—treating others as you want to be treated.